She's everywhere, yet nowhere.

her

Tanish Barnwal

BLUEROSE PUBLISHERS
India | U.K.

Copyright © Tanish Barnwal 2025

All rights reserved by author. No part of this publication may be reproduced, stored in a retrieval system or transmitted in any form or by any means, electronic, mechanical, photocopying, recording or otherwise, without the prior permission of the author. Although every precaution has been taken to verify the accuracy of the information contained herein, the publisher assumes no responsibility for any errors or omissions. No liability is assumed for damages that may result from the use of information contained within.

BlueRose Publishers takes no responsibility for any damages, losses, or liabilities that may arise from the use or misuse of the information, products, or services provided in this publication.

For permissions requests or inquiries regarding this publication, please contact:

BLUEROSE PUBLISHERS
www.BlueRoseONE.com
info@bluerosepublishers.com
+91 8882 898 898
+4407342408967

ISBN: 978-93-6783-479-4

Cover Design: Aman Sharma
Typesetting: Pooja Sharma

First Edition: February 2025

About the Author

Tanish Barnwal, the author of Her, is a 21-year-old student of English Literature and Philosophy at Guru Nanak Khalsa College of Arts, Science, and Commerce.

From an early age, Tanish had a mind bustling with thoughts, though he struggled to find a way to express them. Over time, he discovered the art of pouring his soul into words—a journey that introduced him to the world of literature. Since then, for over four years, writing has been his constant companion and passion.

Tanish's unique writing style resonates deeply with his readers, captivating them with moments of awe and culminating in an emotional crescendo. He holds the belief that "life is too short to experience every emotion," yet aspires to explore and understand them all through his work, hoping one day to bridge the gap between feeling and knowing.

her

*the first gaze said it all. I looked at his smiling face; pure bliss.
I distracted myself to process the moment, I thought it was just an illusion that I could get rid of, but it was more than that, eyes were addictive, lips were seductive still processing but this time running into him laughing and living
this was my first time of
Vodka
Vagabond, kiss.
-rajeshwari*

Table of Emotions.
before her.

1.	In the Darkness of Light.	4
2.	Tomb of my Whiteish Body.	5
3.	The Last Leaf.	6
4.	Vial of Poison.	7
5.	Unearthly Carcass.	8
6.	Prevailing Existence.	9
7.	Altering.	10
8.	Marooned Pain.	11
9.	Despairing, Sulking.	12
10.	Breathing, Choking.	13
11.	Alcove.	14
12.	Skimmed Moon.	15

during her.

1.	Distilled, Relieved.	18
2.	Ode in You.	19
3.	Collision.	20
4.	Rushing Emotions.	21
5.	Chafing Oceans.	22
6.	Sailing, Drowning.	23
7.	Tale of Immersive Beauty.	24
8.	Impious Soul.	25
9.	Dry Leaves.	26
10.	Embers.	27
11.	Normality.	28
12.	Unexplored trails.	29
13.	Parched Fingertips.	30

after her.

1.	Where do I Belong?	34
2.	Smothering Myself.	35
3.	Shaft of Bones.	36
4.	November.	37
5.	Unsettling Sea.	38
6.	Changing lives.	39
7.	Turning into You.	40
8.	Wound.	41
9.	Some Setting of the Sun.	42
10.	Hollow Abyss.	43
11.	Cigarettes of Grief.	44
12.	Jinxed Memory of Yours.	45

before her.

In the darkness of light.

Sulking at seeing myself in the mirror,
thinking over and over that, am I that poisoned?
Poisoned of my own quatervois,
August light was about to surface,
with its all negativity and darkness behind me,
I was running, out of breath, because I wasn't ready to be immobile,
couldn't survive, incinerated,
accepted the death by the darkness of August light,
deceased, in the darkness of light.

Tomb of my whiteish body.

I die, I suffer to die every descending sun,
and mourn to infinite mutiny within my body,
the moist of November rain,
was tendering into the frigid of December,
the running blood glaciated,
the body benumbed,
the breaths were fading away,
Was it the fall?
Or was it the love?
Or was it the tomb of my whiteish body?
I could never know.

The last leaf.

So there was this night, a night of loneliness,
the silence of death,
that night there was some eventual, eventual of something
getting freed, eventual of setting my soul to have infinite
freedom,
freedom from this unwanted body of mine,
there was this pale; lifeless leaf outside the window,
about to fall off,
so fulfilled of everything, can't even hold on to see some more
sunsets.
there came a strong wind took him along with it,
not worrying-nor waiting,
just took him along,
with that last leaf of the tree,
with the last breath of mine,
I left the world, the cruel world.

Vial of poison.

with these noxious thoughts inside my head,
give me a vial of poison,
to demise sooner,
with those every fall,
I broke, and,
scattered into innumerable pieces.
oh, this is it, the end,
end from this infinite pain,
relieve from the pain of eternities,
demised.

Unearthly carcass.

darkness consumes me at its high,
obscuring the twilight of my mind with it's pitch beauty,
I was lost,
trying to breathe, inside this suffocating body of mine,
everything seemed hard,
strangled, reached out,
famine everywhere, left me alone in a mirage of my own,
maybe some last breaths of mine were left,
gasped, struggled.

Now and forever, everything was a hoax
even what I saw was a mirage,
So is my life. my breaths were too,
streaming blood disguised as water,
letting everything out,
*out of my **unearthly carcass**.*

Prevailing existence.

Sometimes I get lost, lost in my thought,
Who am I? What do I consist of?
am I the concoction of hundreds of books I have read, or the
sum of indefinable souls I have met,
I feel,
everyone out there is an imitation of someone,
someone who left a mark in the world of their presence.

Altering.

How much do we lose of ourselves, everyday,
to attain peace within,
Are we gonna be the same like we used to be in the beginning?
or someone who's tormentingly unrecognisable?

Marooned pain.

It was just pain left,
tears streaming down my face,
and eyes turning red,
Was it love fading away?
or, my flaccid heart?

Despairing, sulking.

All I could think was of demise,
some gruesome end to this unwanted life of mine,
never intended to be something, like I see of myself today,
with no hope to see another rising sun,
or the drowning moon,
despairing, sulking over what I had dreamt of becoming.

Breathing, choking.

Aren't we all thriving on the edge of breathing-choking,
Which is contrasting into a lie now,
a hoax of forever?

Alcove.

It feels like an alcove,
where its hard to breath,
a space where it rain melancholically,
and sometimes,
I deny to be this demeanour,
never seeked to turn into something lifeless,
something more like a carcass,
but in the end.
Aren't we all turning into dried leaves?

Skimmed Moon.

how much do the moon get skimmed by grazing,
to attain something new, <u>unobtrusive</u> side,
And then to garnering something from nothing, from
something new,
obscured into something whole,
something complete.

during her.

Distilled, relieved.

I respired every ounce of you,
felt all of you,
then I let you dissolve in me,
I distilled, I relived,
a blend of you and me,
emerged thoughts and love.

Ode in you.

with one touch it was shivered,
With just one glance of yours,
and I made you mine,
I felt you,
this time not just in the green fields but for real,
For some junctures, I was lost,
in your pale brown-hazel eyes,
I saw an ode in you,
the deep one, where I get all my pleasures,
the intimidating word pleasures.

Collision.

when our firth chafed onto each other,
felt like never before,
that lust to create that liaison,
that hold of your lips into my neck,
those filthy hands-into-hands,
like it's been glued together,
and then at a glance all desires,
came into reality, which can be seen with naked eyes,
which can be felt by the collision of two mortals.

Rushing emotions.

rushing emotions to lips,
forcing one another's body in crashing into each other's souls,
interwoven lips,
expressing love through pleasures,
followed by sensual actions.

Chafing Oceans.

coarseness of the lips,
covet of pulling you into arms,
the raucous of my fingertips grazing over your bosoms, your
abated breaths, arduous breaths, making me to chisel myself
into you,
and let our firth chafe onto each other, like emerging oceans.

Sailing, drowning.

My love will sail,
It will sail all seven oceans, to drown in your infinite love,
going through storms and thunder,
for that one held of time,
for that one kiss of water,
for that one drown in your love,
With your love, demise in your love.

Tale of an Immersive Beauty.

The smile was enough to hold an eye on you,
Those lips had a lot to recite but were held on.
Thou's light brown eyes were adequate to astray,
soul like a sunflower, charming forever.
the vulnerable you, was attractive,
because it was ineffable.
Was it even real or a tale of an immersive beauty?

Impious soul.

if you wish to be with me,
you've to drown in the unholy blood of mine,
have to kiss me at my low,
but for that, you've to be mine,
you've to accept me in my darkest,
you've to bewitch my impious soul,
and, if you do all of it,
I will mortgage my soul, and my body to you,
to only you.

Dry leaves.

Her eyes raced to catch mine in the crowd of 100s
my lips clasping for that one word to be uttered to her,
while our forged feelings crash,
Suddenly it feels like an eternity because we seem to be lost
within the bury time and shadows.
knowing the fact of never seeing her again and got me
unstable but, isn't that the reality,
aren't we all gonna be strangers one day?

Embers.

I love you as wood do to fire,
Burning in embers without worrying about turning into ash.

Normality.

I think that i am losing my mind,
it doesn't feel like it use to before,
angst, disorientated.
i think i am losing myself,
it's not that loud in my head anymore,
i've got a hold on calmness, now, when i close my eyes i don't
hear 100s of echoes, now all that i listen is birds chirping and
rain drizzling down on leaves, waves crashing to the shore,
Is that what I am supposed to feel?
Does this feel like going demented?
Or am I just coming to my normality?

Unexplored trails.

parched fingertips, running across my neck,
like it's the un-gazed trails,
eye con-coursing like have been on halt for an era,
bodies emerging, prone to each other,
dune to moist clouds.
rain to barren land.

Parched fingertips.

Moment when you lay down a finger of yours on the naked body of mine,
you in-flame a fire which kept scorching until you cease to be visible,
and soon that you happen to retrieve, it turns all into pale; lifeless,
and soon my skin had turned parched,
parched like burning paper turning into ash.

after her.

Where do I belong?

Now you tell me where I belong?
whether in the dark abyss, or
in the obscurity of death,
all of me was fading,
breathes were shortening,
eyes were clasping,
oh thou, tell me where do i belong?
whether in the unholiness of dawn, or
in the bury of time,
the cruel ray of January were passing,
and, February was about to appear with its pain and
torturing towards my soul.
Where do I belong?

Smothering myself.

If i could, i would smother myself to decease with the bolster under my head,
because the will to see another dawn have been obscured,
the feeling of living inside of a walking flesh hadn't been finished,
even if i move my eye around, it would get thunked on the abyss i am unaware of,
abyss which were dark and hollow and is incessant like the pain within me.

Shaft of Bones.

What have you turned me into?
just a shaft of bones and flesh accumulated all together,
no sensations, no feelings,
Is that how you found me?
or is that how I have become after your disappearance?

November.

your memories are deeply engraved within me like carving on a tree bark,
Is that what you thought you'd do?
was that your true intentions; to leave me broken for eternity,
the frigidness of November have become mellow,
and the January light isn't that cruel anymore,
the blood within me isn't that bright anymore, it's pale,
It's like the shedding of maple leaves in winter.
I wish, and i kept wishing that one day,
you will come and pour the water of our love on the famine'd tree of mine.

Unsettling Sea.

and what is that you look for in an unsettling ocean?
Whether the instability or the peace in the sound of crashing waves to shore,
What is that you seek when you're at your lowest?
What is it that you feel in the depth of your coarse heart when you miss them?
is it someone to fill in the voids,
or reconciling the beauty of voids within.

Changing lives.

necessity will soon form into needs,
wanting may turn into cravings,
thoughts shall ripe into fledgling hope,
everything has to change as per the oscillation of the
pendulum of life,
but, this never ending hatred in the delves of my coarse heart
will never desuetude until it beats.

Turning into you.

Tell me what have you done to me?
i still feel your breath lying next to me,
your eyes abodes me, like shadow to sun,
that moment when our firth rubbed against each other,
they just exchanged something, maybe traded a soul,
or, ploughed a seed of your outgrown love in me,
which kept sprouting unless it consumed all of me,
eaten all of me, hitherto i altered into you,
until I turned into you,
An incomplete you.

Wound.

the rosewood fret just outboard'd,
the metal string left unhinged, cutting through the pale skin
of mine,
leaving enough of a parched-flaccid skin of mine,
deep enough to leave a wound on my soul,
and just the way, it was left out of tune.

Some setting of the sun.

and maybe someday there will be some setting of the sun,
where, i will be fulfilled of everything,
where, i will be able to think as i should,
where, i think i have achieved everything,
where, i will finally be able rest my legs from infinite running,
But, will I really be able to?
Will I really be able to accept it? the way it is,
Will there be such a sunset?
or will I be still mourning about the voids I have within?

Hollow Abyss.

Why do I feel agonised?
and the distinctive echo due to hollowness,
the pain within me doesn't seem to be fading, or
maybe it obscured by gentle rays of the moon above me,
the fear of letting go, the soreness of holding on-to it, have
gotten me irritably melancholic,
why is that, feeling your presence was a mere disaster, which
left me scattered all over, again
maybe the contentment will rise as I lose the hold on-to your
memories within me, like the setting moon moving on to the
horizon and then vanishing.

Cigarettes of Grief

I do not know how many cigarettes of grief,
have been burnt in my parched fingers to get over the thought,
the thought of you never reappearing in the poisoned life of
mine.

Jinxed memory of yours.

I will find a way, way to live with the jinxed memories of yours,
because when ere morning will draw nigh,
you'll fade away.
I knew, whatever comes together,
parts away
But loving you was never a burden to me.
I will find a way to live without you,
because when you cede on me so calmly,
and to those infinite love of ours,
which got shattered in seconds,
which made me doubt my own entity,
makes me think that I was never good enough for someone to understand
thou, will find a way to live in the incomplete liaison of ours,
because I was a fiend of your abridged love
love, which left stranded
I was not ready to see my existence getting evanescent from your life,
from the same eyes which were dreaming of our eventual closely
thou, will find a way to live without me,
Because my existence never mattered to you,
nor my love did
And when the sun will arise and I won't be there to be with you
To stop that tear streaming down your face. To hold on to you.

They say eventually everything decays,
so shall your memories.

The end.

www.ingramcontent.com/pod-product-compliance
Lightning Source LLC
LaVergne TN
LVHW061631070526
838199LV00071B/6647